WELCOME TO

Beast Quest

Collect the special coins in this book.
You will earn one gold coin for
every chapter you read.

Once you have finished all the chapters,
find out what to do with your gold coins at
the back of the book.

With special thanks to Tabitha Jones

For Ewan Beverley, Sienna Lowery and Reuben Lowery

www.beastquest.co.uk

ORCHARD BOOKS

First published in Great Britain in 2018 by The Watts Publishing Group

1 3 5 7 9 10 8 6 4 2

Text © 2018 Beast Quest Limited.
Cover and inside illustrations by Steve Sims
© Beast Quest Limited 2018

Beast Quest is a registered trademark of Beast Quest Limited
Series created by Beast Quest Limited, London

A CIP catalogue record for this book is available from the British Library.

ISBN 978 1 40834 336 4

Printed in Great Britain

The paper and board used in this book are made from wood from responsible sources

Orchard Books
An imprint of Hachette Children's Group
Part of The Watts Publishing Group Limited
Carmelite House, 50 Victoria Embankment, London EC4Y 0DZ

An Hachette UK Company
www.hachette.co.uk
www.hachettechildrens.co.uk

Beast Quest®

MenoX
THE SABRE-TOOTHED
TERROR

BY ADAM BLADE

ORCHARD

MAKAI

REDSTEEL FORGE

THE
ELIXIR
WELLS

CONTENTS

Quake before me, Avantians. You think you are safe in your distant kingdom, but you couldn't be more wrong.

All of Makai is under my control. This island's ancient Beasts are risen again and obey my every word. The people are my slaves, building a force unlike any you've ever seen. I will do what my mother, Kensa, and my father, Sanpao, never could...I will have vengeance on Tom and his people.

You can muster your soldiers. You can assemble your navy. But you will never be ready.

I'll be seeing you very soon.

Your soon-to-be ruler,

Ria

CELEBRATIONS CUT SHORT

Tom and Elenna pressed through the throng of brightly dressed partygoers crowding the palace courtyard. They passed jugglers, fortune-tellers, jesters and countless traders calling out from behind market stalls piled high with delicious food or handmade wares.

The cheerful melody of pipes
and bells filled the square, and
everywhere Tom looked he could
see the smiling faces of townsfolk
celebrating the safe return of the
royal family to the palace.

At the palace doors, a pair of
guards waved Tom and Elenna
inside. King Hugo and Queen Aroha
sat in state in the throne room, their
jewelled crowns glittering in the
morning sun that slanted through

the open windows. Aroha gently
rocked Prince Thomas's wicker
cradle on a wooden stand at her side.
Behind the royal family, Daltec the
wizard stood with his mentor, Aduro,
both wearing matching dark blue
robes covered in stars and moons.

"We've brought gifts for baby
Thomas," Elenna said.

"How kind of you!" Queen Aroha
said.

Tom and Elenna peered into the
cradle. Baby Thomas stared up
at them with round blue eyes, his
pudgy fists pumping as if he were
fighting an imaginary opponent.
"Here you go, Tommy, this is for you,"
Elenna said, holding a driftwood

carving of a wolf towards the child.
The baby gurgled and made a jab for
the toy, almost knocking it from her
hand.

"He's getting strong!" Elenna said,

placing the gift beside the baby. Tom lifted the present he'd brought – a soft black cushion stitched in the shape of a stallion. His aunt had made it for him when he was a baby, and he remembered playing with its soft tassels and shiny button eyes. *I hope he likes it!* As Tom leaned over the cot to set his cushion next to Elenna's wolf, baby Thomas let out a squeak and swung his tiny fist, bopping Tom right on the nose.

"Ow!" Tom reeled back in surprise, his eyes watering from the blow.

"Ha!" Hugo said, smiling proudly.

Suddenly, angry shouting rose above the music and laughter drifting through the windows.

"This way, you scoundrel!" Booted feet stomped along the passageway outside, quickly followed by a heavy rap on the door.

"Come in!" Hugo called, but even before the words were out the chamber door burst open and Admiral Ryker strode through, his chin lifted high as he saluted the king.

"I bring important news!" Ryker cried. Two uniformed officers dragged a sun-browned man wearing tattered rags into the room. The captive's shirt had been torn, showing his ribs; a stubbly beard covered his hollow cheeks. His pale, bloodshot eyes looked wild with fear.

"We apprehended this vagabond after he washed up on the southwestern shore," Ryker said.

The admiral tugged up the prisoner's sleeve, revealing a black pirate skull on the red-brown skin. "He's a spy for the Pirates of Makai."

The captive man flinched. "I'm no pirate!" he croaked. "I was fleeing Makai. The pirates have—"

"Silence!" Ryker shouted.

Tom glanced at the mark on the man's arm and frowned. "King Hugo," he said, "that mark is no tattoo. It's a brand. I think we should hear this man out."

The captive man nodded vigorously, his eyes flicking between Tom and the king.

"Let him speak," Hugo told Ryker.

"But…" Ryker started to protest,

but Hugo silenced him with a stern look. The admiral let the man go.

"Life's always been hard on Makai," said the prisoner, "what with Sanpao's pirates looting and taking their cut of everything – but now his daughter Ria's in charge, it's a thousand times worse. She's got all Sanpao's men working for her and she won't rest until she's taken control of everything and everyone."

Ryker let out a loud sniff. "Ridiculous," he scoffed. "I've seen this Ria. How can a skinny girl take control of a whole kingdom?"

"She managed to sink most of your navy," Elenna muttered.

Ryker opened and shut his mouth,

a fierce blush spreading up his cheeks. "I…"

"Go on," King Hugo told the captive.

"The folk of Makai aren't normally ones to beg," the prisoner said, "but that's what I've come here for. On behalf of all our men, women and children – we need help, and we need it quickly. Sanpao's lass has four Beasts under her control. We don't stand a chance."

Tom's pulse quickened.

"Four Beasts?" Daltec said, from his place behind the king and queen. "I didn't think there were any Beasts on Makai."

"There were, three hundred years

ago," Aduro said, looking grave. It had been a long time since he had been drained of his magic, but the former wizard knew more about the history of Beasts and kingdoms than anyone else. "And from this man's story, it sounds like they have risen again. Makai was once a prosperous kingdom, but Eris, a powerful sorceress of old, summoned four Beasts which all but wiped out the population. Four neighbouring kingdoms sent Mistresses and Masters of Beasts to their aid. The Beasts were vanquished, and a magical token taken from each. However, Eris took her revenge on the victors. As they returned home, she sank their ships and the tokens too. Everyone aboard perished." Aduro shook his head sorrowfully. "It was a terrible, terrible time. It sounds like Ria must somehow have recovered the four tokens and returned them to the vanquished Beasts in order to reawaken them. A reckless and foolish act – but sadly just the sort thing we might expect from the child of Sanpao and Kensa."

"We must go and help the people of Makai at once!" Elenna said.

"I don't see why," Ryker snapped. "They're nothing but a bunch of thugs and pirates. They can look after themselves."

His prisoner let out a mirthless chuckle. "We're not the only ones in danger," he said. "Ria is building an attack fleet as we speak – enslaving the whole population of Makai to help. Then she will turn her attention to Avantia."

The room hushed, and Tom felt an icy prickle of fear.

Ryker reddened. "Impossible. Makai is three days' sailing over treacherous seas – her fleet will not survive the journey!"

The prisoner nodded. "But her ships won't be on the waves. They'll be flying!"

King Hugo gasped. "All of them?"

The prisoner nodded gravely. "Ria

has hundreds working at the Elixir Wells – the source of the fuel that makes ships float."

Tom swallowed. He'd encountered Sanpao's flying vessel in the past. It was hard enough to deal with one ship, but a whole fleet…

"Elenna and I will go," he declared. "Ria must be stopped."

Ryker adjusted his tricorn hat and cleared his throat. "Um…well…I should stay here, of course," he said. "To, er…oversee the rebuilding of the navy."

Daltec shot the admiral a chilly look. "I'll accompany Tom and Elenna," he told the king. "Ria is a powerful sorceress, like her mother.

It is likely they will need magical
assistance. However, I can't get them
all the way using magic – it's too far.
We will need at least one ship."

Tom noticed Admiral Ryker shifting uncomfortably, but before he could make another excuse, Elenna chimed in.

"Don't worry," she said, "I know a man who can take us there, discreetly." She shot Ryker a look. "And he won't be put off by the mention of a few Beasts."

1

THE ISLAND OF MAKAI

"Land ahoy!" Elenna cried, leaping up from her place beside Tom on a narrow bench and pointing out over the glittering blue-green waves. Tom rose too, feeling the deck lurch beneath him. He spotted a dark smudge shimmering in a heat haze on the horizon.

Makai!

"At last!" Daltec croaked, looking green. They had been squashed together aboard Elenna's uncle Leo's tiny sloop for three days. Daltec had spent most of that time bent over the side as the small ship rolled on the choppy water. Tom hadn't enjoyed the journey much more. Having to sit idle while he knew that Ria was wreaking havoc in Makai made him feel like he might explode with frustration.

As they neared the island, Tom spotted a wide curved bay with a wooden quay, overlooked by tiers of ramshackle buildings, tightly packed together along the waterfront like crooked teeth.

"Keep quiet and look as mean as you can from here on in," Leo said, his hands moving deftly on the rigging as he guided them into

the dock. "From what I've heard of Makai, you're going to need to blend in with a rough crowd."

Waves slapped gently at the harbour wall and tatty boats with peeling paint bobbed alongside the jetty. Tom felt a prickle of dread as he scanned the streets and buildings beyond. Something was very wrong. Apart from a few gulls wheeling overhead, the whole place looked deserted.

"Where is everyone?" Elenna asked, echoing his thoughts. "Isn't this supposed to be a lawless fishing port full of pirates and traders?"

Tom shivered despite the heat.

"Whatever's going on, I expect Ria

has something to do with it," he said. "And she'll be lying in wait for us somewhere. We'll have to keep our wits about us."

Leo angled the sailboat into the wind, slowing it sharply as he brought it alongside the jetty. Elenna hopped off to tie the mooring line. Tom buckled on his sword then leapt down beside her, followed closely by Daltec. The young wizard wore a lightweight brown tunic and trousers rather than his cloak. The folk of Makai distrusted magic, and Aduro had cautioned Daltec to stay disguised and not to use his powers unless absolutely necessary.

As Leo adjusted the rigging to set

sail once more, Elenna untied the mooring. "Make sure you come back in one piece!" Leo called to her, then he gave Tom and Daltec a salute, before cutting away through the waves.

Tom, Elenna and Daltec strode towards the fishing port, their footsteps knocking on the wooden jetty. Dark, empty windows greeted them, and doors hanging wide on broken hinges. Apart from the gentle hush of the sea, the only sounds were the creak of a signboard swinging in the breeze and the squawk of gulls squabbling over a heel of bread. They passed discarded lobster pots, coiled ropes and stacks of sailcloth beside storage barrels. Everything you would expect to see in a busy port, except any sign of a living person.

"This place is starting to give me the creeps," Elenna said in a hushed voice.

"Let's look inside," Tom said. He put his hand on the hilt of his sword and led Daltec and Elenna into a tavern. Even in the shadowy gloom, he could see at once that some sort of struggle had taken place. Upturned tables and broken chairs lay strewn about. Broken glass littered the floor, which felt tacky underfoot from spilled ale.

"Anyone there?" Daltec shouted. Tom spotted a movement from the corner of his eye and tightened his grip on his sword. He turned to see a dark shape slink from the shadows beneath a table. *A cat.* The creature arched its back and hissed angrily at Daltec, then stalked away through the open door.

Daltec let out a nervous laugh. "Shame it can't tell us where everyone's gone," he said. "I suppose we should press further inland." They followed the cat out into daylight. Tom lifted his hand against the glare, when he heard a shuffling sound from above and spun. Daltec let out a yelp as a heavy net dropped over them. The ropes tightened, crushing Elenna and Daltec against Tom. The net jerked and all three landed in a tangled heap. He craned his neck to see two huge figures bent over them – a broad man with a head shaved except for a single braid, and an even broader woman with a matted tangle of black hair and dark, scowling eyes. Tattoos covered their sun-browned faces.

Pirates!

"Where've you been hiding, you workshy landlubber scum?" the woman bellowed.

The man let out a grunt of disgust, then spat. "They're only young'uns!" he said. He leaned down so low, Tom could smell his rotten breath. "Found some weapons to play with, have you?" he said. "I could

show you a game or two." He grinned, showing crooked yellow teeth, and lifted his cutlass. Elenna squirmed, trying to break off an arrowhead over her shoulder, but Tom nudged her in the ribs. "We don't want to blow our cover!" he hissed in her ear. Elenna fell still.

"Don't hurt us!" Tom said, in a high shaky voice. "We were just mucking about. We didn't mean any trouble."

"Ha! Well, trouble's exactly what you've now got," the man with the crooked teeth said. "Ria says it's all hands on deck. You're coming with us, and you're going to work like everyone else. It's either that, or a long walk off a short jetty. Choice is yours!"

REDSTEEL FORGE

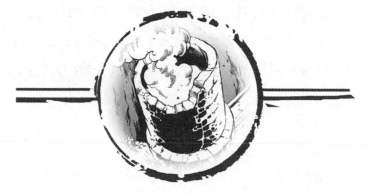

Tom sat squashed between Elenna and Daltec in the back of an open, rickety cart. Beyond the thick neck and shaven skull of the pirate in the driving seat, Tom could see a winding dirt track, climbing steeply up the side of a rocky, barren mountain. With every bump and jolt of the cart, rusty manacles chafed his ankles. The sun burned down from above, making his skin feel tight and sore, but the heat was nothing compared to the rage that burned in his belly as he listened to their captors' chatter.

"It hardly seems worth bringing in such puny runts as these," said the big man holding the reins, "but I guess Ria will know how to get a decent day's work out of them."

The woman next to him chuckled. "Aye, right enough. Between her whip and her Beasts, she gets stuff done. I reckon our fortunes are on the way up with her in charge. She's a lot more likely to make us rich than her father was, that's for sure."

"Ha! Especially now – I heard Sanpao ended up as dinner for some Beast or other."

"That's what I heard too," the woman said. "I suppose Ria must take after her mother – you'd never catch Kensa winding up inside a Beast!"

"You're right there," the driver said. "If anyone can pull off a proper raid on Avantia, it's going to be Ria. Just think of all the looting and feasting there'll be."

Tom clenched his fists. *There won't be any...not while there's blood in my veins...*

As the cart trundled onwards along the rocky path, Tom heard new sounds over the creak of the wheels and the clop of the mule's hooves. First, the familiar echoing chime of hammers – lots of hammers – hitting steel, then groans and weak cries of pain. He made out the familiar hiss of hot metal dunked in water, and the crack of a whip. Soon the acrid stench of burning caught in his throat. As they neared the mountain's peak, he could see plumes of smoke rising into the sky, mingling with the clouds. *There's some sort of forge...*

They crested the top of the mountain and started a steep descent down a narrow winding path. Tom gasped at what lay below. Elenna let out a small cry of dismay. It looked like a great chunk had been gouged out of the mountainside, leaving a scarred curve of cliff-face, pock-marked with tunnels. At the base of the cliff, partly surrounded by the high rock walls of the mountainside, sprawled what looked like a huge, open-air metalworks.

Wooden carts piled with black ore streaked with scarlet ran on tracks from the tunnels. People in rags toiled in the sun, unloading the carts and breaking the rocks with pick-axes and mallets. At the centre of the busy space, a vast, chimney-shaped furnace surrounded by wooden scaffolding belched smoke into the sky.

Workers near the base of the tower operated huge sets of leather bellows. Others unloaded buckets of ore from platforms suspended from

a complex pulley system, and tipped them into the furnace.

Bright molten metal flowed from spouts at the base of the tower, gushing like fiery floodwater. Lines of workers passed crucibles of melted ore from the tower to nearby benches where blacksmiths cast and hammered swords, while others poured the liquid metal into moulds to make arrowheads and spear-tips.

Every worker in the vast human machine looked sick and malnourished, but all moved at a frantic pace. And Tom could see why. Tattooed pirates brandishing canes and whips slouched between them, barking orders and landing unearned blows on the workers' scarred and sunburned skin.

Tom felt a cold, sick horror creep over him. *Ria's enslaved the whole population of Makai!*

"Whoa!" The pirate driving pulled the mules to a stop at the base of the cliff. He swung from his seat and strode to the back of the cart. "Welcome to Redsteel Forge," he said with an ugly smirk. The dark-haired woman climbed down to stand before Tom, Elenna and Daltec in the cart.

"Off!" she barked, shoving Tom backwards on to the ground and then doing the same to Elenna and Daltec. They scrambled up as fast as they could with their manacled feet. Tom turned to see a huge pirate with a hollow scar in place of an eye marching towards them. *One-Eye!* Tom remembered him only too well from previous Quests fighting Sanpao and his crew. One-Eye was one of the most ruthless and cruel of the lot. Tom quickly smeared the dirt from his hands across his face, and nudged Elenna to do the same, before lowering his gaze.

"Got some fresh blood here for you," their crooked-toothed captor told One-Eye.

The huge pirate scowled, running his gaze over Tom, Elenna and Daltec. "Not much muscle on 'em,

but I suppose they'll do," he said.
"You!" he barked at Daltec. "You're
the puniest of the lot. Over to the
furnace. You can work the bellows."
The big pirate frowned down at
Elenna. He jerked a thumb towards
a breaking station near a tunnel
mouth where slaves unloaded ore
from carts then smashed it apart
in teams. "Over there. Get moving."
While Elenna hobbled away, One-
Eye turned to Tom and frowned. "Do
I know you from somewhere?" the
pirate asked.

"I don't think so, sir," Tom
mumbled, keeping his head down.
"I'm a blacksmith's son. I'm ready
to work, and I know how to forge a

blade." As Tom spoke, he noticed an iron key hanging from the big man's belt – it looked the right size to fit the manacles clamped about his ankles.

"Well, you've come to the right place," One-Eye said. He tipped his head towards a bench crowded with blacksmiths. "We'll work you until you can't lift that arm any more."

Tom put on a pair of leather gloves and started work on a sword. The grey-haired man beside him was awkwardly hunched over, but he hammered away with practised skill, powerful muscles standing out on his sinewy arms.

"Thirsty work!" Tom said. "Where

do we get water?"

The man turned to gape at him, the whites of his eyes showing as his gaze darted nervously about him. "No water, except at dawn, noon and sundown," he hissed. "And no talking or you'll get a whipping. Or worse." The old man's wandering gaze suddenly fixed on something behind Tom. His face paled and he went back to work, hammering harder and faster than before. Tom glanced over his shoulder and spotted what had frightened the man. A little way off, a slender girl dressed in shining armour, the same bright scarlet as her mohawk hair, stalked between the workers. A crackling cat-o'-nine-

tails trailed from her hand. *Ria!* Tom noticed how the workers quickened their pace, their backs stiff and their eyes fixed on their work. Even the pirate overseers seemed to tense, avoiding Ria's gaze as she strode past.

She's coming my way! Tom realised, dropping his gaze. He heard the click of her boots stop right behind him and swallowed hard.

"You're not doing too badly for such a scrawny little thing," Ria said. "I can almost see some muscle on that skinny arm. What's your name?" Tom's stomach tightened. His gaze flicked to the half-finished blade in his hand – but knew it wouldn't match Ria's whip. He thought of the brawny pirates all around them, and the heavy manacles on his legs. *I can't fight them all...and if she works out who I am, this Quest is over before it's even begun!*

4

FEEDING THE BEAST

Tom kept his eyes on the bench in front of him, feeling a sweat breaking out across his body that was nothing to do with the heat in the forge. "Name's, uh...Peter," he mumbled.

"Hmmm," Ria said. Tom could feel her gaze boring into him. "That's an unusual accent you've got there. Where are you from?"

Tom swallowed. "I'm —"

An echoing clang rang out above the hammering and clattering of the forge, followed by a yelp. Tom looked up to see a wizened, ancient-looking man backing away from a pool of scarlet metal spilling from a fallen crucible. The metal smoked on the ground, already hardening. The slaves either side of him quickly drew away from the mess, closing the gap in the line, then continued their work.

"Fool!" Ria snarled. "Wasting my redsteel! Bring him to me!" The old man started to shake, his knees knocking together so hard he could barely stand. A huge pirate with a bushy black beard marched over to him, grabbed his arm and dragged him to Ria, throwing him down at her feet. The man knelt, head bowed and shoulders trembling.

"Please, mistress! Please don't hurt me, it was an accident," he said. Ria lifted her crackling whip. Tom winced as the old man cringed lower, shielding his head with his arms.

"Actually…" Ria said, in a quiet, thoughtful voice that chilled Tom to the bone, "I've changed my mind." She lowered her whip.

The man at her feet sagged with relief. "Thank you, mistress, thank you!" he said, pawing at her boots.

Ria lifted her gaze to the bearded pirate behind him. "You!" she snapped. "This is your fault. You obviously haven't been hard enough on the workers – letting them make stupid mistakes." She gestured to One-Eye, who was leaning against the wooden beam of a scaffold nearby, picking his teeth. "Take him to Menox!" Ria cried. "And let this be a lesson to all of you!"

The bearded pirate put up his hands and shook his head, eyes wide with fear. "No!" he cried, backing away as One-Eye strode towards him. "Ria! Please! I'll do anything you want. I've been part of this crew since before you were born. I served your old pa half my life."

Ria's face darkened. "Well, Sanpao's gone now, fool," she spat. "I'm in charge!" She turned with a toss of her head, and strode away.

One-Eye lifted his cutlass, smirking. The bearded pirate took another step back, hitting a bench behind him. A clanking rattle started up from across the worksite, and Tom looked to see a massive, bare-chested man sitting high on a raised wooden platform near the base of the cliff, turning the handle of a winch. The pirate grunted with effort as he hauled up a thick metal chain attached to one side of a huge wooden panel on the ground. One edge of the panel started to lift, revealing the inky darkness of a gaping pit. An angry snarling sound echoed up from the shadows.

"Boss! Please, no!" the pirate cried, his face blotchy and his lips flecked with spit. One-Eye simply grinned, dipped his shoulder and bundled the man on to his back. The pirate kicked and struggled as One-Eye carried him to the pit.

"Argh!" he cried, as One-Eye leaned over and dropped him into the darkness. A hungry snarl echoed up at once, followed by a terrified scream. Tom felt cold with horror when the scream was cut off with a

muffled yelp. One-Eye dusted off his
hands and walked away after Ria.

*What in all the kingdoms is down
there?* Tom wondered.

5

FIGHT!

Tom caught Elenna's gaze across the
worksite and gestured towards One-
Eye. The big man was passing close
to Elenna's breaking station as he
followed Ria towards a mine tunnel.
Tom pointed to the manacles around
Elenna's ankles and mimed turning
a key. Elenna glanced towards the
pirate. Tom saw her eyes widen as

they fixed on the heavy key hanging from the side of his belt. She turned back to Tom with a determined look and nodded. Tom nodded back. Time to shake things up!

Tom gasped as Elenna's eyes rolled up in her head, her knees buckled and she collapsed heavily against an ore cart. For a second he thought she was sick, then he realised… *She's acting!* One-Eye let out a growl and stormed towards Elenna, brandishing his club. But before the big man could take a swing at her, Elenna snatched up a chunk of ore that had fallen from the cart, whipped back her arm and flung the rock. *CRACK!* One-Eye put his

hands to his forehead, groaning in pain. Elenna ducked behind him, shoving him hard in the base of the spine. *Go, Elenna!* The scarred pirate staggered forwards and pitched headfirst into the cart, his booted legs kicking out behind him. Elenna leapt to his side, unclipped the key from his belt, then gave the ore cart a push. With a clatter of wheels, it started moving, rolling back along its metal tracks, quickly disappearing into darkness.

After shooting Tom a thumbs-up, Elenna quickly glanced about, then bent to unlock her manacles. Tom turned towards the furnace, seeing Daltec already hobbling towards him carrying an armful of clay moulds. The wizard winked.

Elenna hurried across the steelworks, ducking between benches and scaffolds as she went. "Nice work!" Tom said when she reached him and Daltec. "You even had me fooled."

Elenna grinned. "That was the easy bit," she said. "Now, somehow, we have to get our weapons and fight that Beast!"

Elenna quickly unfastened Tom and Daltec's shackles, then pressed the key into the hand of a young slave girl nearby. "Free anyone you can," Elenna told her. The girl eagerly agreed, staring wide-eyed at the key.

Tom turned to Daltec and tipped his head towards the cart they had arrived in. "Do you think you can create a diversion while we fetch our weapons?" he asked.

Daltec nodded, "I've been studying the workings of the furnace – I think I know just the thing. Good luck," he said, then started back towards the huge furnace at the centre of the worksite, still hobbling as if his feet were tied.

Tom and Elenna dived in the other direction, heading for the cart at the foot of the mountain. They hurried from bench to bench, hunched low to the ground, keeping out of sight as much as possible. Up ahead, Tom spotted a pair of familiar bulky forms striding between the workers. A broad man with a thick neck and shaven head alongside a huge woman with a tangle of black hair – the pirates that had captured them. The man swung his whip as he passed a small boy, lashing the child across the shoulders. The boy let out a yelp of pain. The pirates laughed and strode on. Tom and Elenna exchanged a steely nod of agreement, picked up hefty chunks of ore, and charged. *Thunk! Crack!* The two pirates sank to their knees, then pitched forward on to their faces, knocked out cold.

Tom and Elenna skirted around the fallen pirates and raced on. Measuring the short distance to the cart with his eyes, Tom felt a surge of hope. *We can do this!* Then – *BOOF!* A red flash flooded his vision as pain exploded inside his skull. Tom turned, reeling slightly with dizziness to see the man with hunched shoulders from his bench scowling back at him, holding a wooden mallet.

"What are you doing?" Elenna cried.

"I'm saving our skins is what I'm doing," the man growled. "Turning against Ria is suicide. You can get yourselves killed if you like, but you're not taking the rest of us down with you." Through his spinning vision, Tom spotted two lanky young pirates marching towards them, carrying whips.

"Get back to work!" one of the pirates shouted. Suddenly a tremendous fizzing, whooshing noise drowned out all other sounds. Everyone turned. Bright yellow

flames were shooting from an open
door halfway up the side of the
furnace tower, and smoke billowed
out in clouds. Daltec stood on the
platform beside the open door
shielding his face from the heat

with his arms. Glowing molten rock
spurted into a vat at his side.

"Stop him!" a gruff voice cried
from somewhere nearby. The smoke
quickly spread to cover the whole
site, making the workers cough.

"Run!" Tom told Elenna as a black cloud enveloped them, hiding them from view. He covered his mouth and nose with his sleeve and started off through the thick dark smoke in the direction of the cart. Elenna's shadowy form kept pace beside him, and angry cries rang out from every direction.

"Close those doors!"

"Get that man!"

As the smoke started to clear, Tom spotted the cart only paces away. He and Elenna leapt into it. They grabbed their weapons, then crouched, hidden, peering out at the chaos around them. Through the thinning smoke haze, Tom could see the furnace doors had been shut, but he couldn't spot Daltec.

"What's going on?" Ria cried, striding from the mouth of a tunnel, her whip raised and her face contorted with fury. All the slaves, even those who had been freed, immediately snapped to their work stations, heads down and hands busy.

A harsh male voice answered Ria. "This lousy slop-pot opened the furnace's slag outlet." Tom squinted through the smoke in the direction of the voice to see two tall young pirates, both dressed from head to toe in black, holding Daltec by the arms. The two men half carried, half dragged Daltec towards Ria and held

him up before her.

"I know him!" a female voice piped up. Tom looked to see a slender woman with garish green hair and a nose-ring scowling at Daltec across the worksite. "He's one of Hugo's pet wizards."

"Is he now…?" Ria said. Daltec flinched as she leaned in close to his face, looking hard into his wide, terrified eyes. "What would Hugo's wizard be doing here?"

"I…I'm no wizard," Daltec stammered. "I'm just a fisherman. I don't know no spells or nothing like that."

"A fisherman?" Ria spat. "With that soft skin and those skinny arms! Rot! You're a spy!"

"Mistress!" a low, gruff voice called out from the shadow of the mountain. Tom looked over to see One-Eye stride from a tunnel, a huge purple lump on his forehead. "Tom and Elenna are here somewhere!"

A slow smile spread across Ria's face. "Are they, indeed?" she said. "Then this wizard must belong to them. Take him to Menox's pit," she told her men, then strode towards the gaping hole in the ground. The young pirates dragged Daltec after her. When they reached the edge of the pit, Ria turned to gaze out over the metalworks, still smiling. "Come out, come out, wherever you are!" she called in a sing song voice. Then her smile vanished, and her voice lowered to a furious growl. "Right now! Or your wizard friend dies!"

Tom and Elenna leapt from the

cart, weapons held in front of them.

"So nice of you to visit," Ria said, her green eyes flashing with spite as they fixed on Tom and Elenna. "It will make invading Avantia so much easier for me once I've fed you and your friend here to the Beast."

"Let him go!" Elenna said.

Ria shrugged. "If you insist," she said. Then she stepped forwards and shoved Daltec in the chest. *No!* The wizard's arms windmilled for a moment as he tried to catch his balance, his eyes round with fear.

Then he toppled back into the pit.

1

BEAST PIT

Tom set off at a run, his sword and shield raised. He heard Elenna's arrow whizz past him just as Ria dived behind one of her men, using him like a shield. The arrow clattered against the ground, and Elenna let out a growl of frustration.

"Have fun!" Ria called, peeking

out from behind her black-clad crewmate. Then she ducked away through the crowd and vanished down a mine tunnel.

Tom could barely contain the fury burning in his chest, but he had to stay focussed. Daltec's life depended on it. He could hear hungry snarls and snuffling sounds echoing from the pit. As Tom raced onwards, a dozen pirates leapt towards him. He dodged through lashing whips and smashed aside swinging blades without breaking his stride.

Suddenly, a group of huge tattooed men wielding clubs and cutlasses formed a line before him, blocking his way. Tom let out a cry

and charged onwards, sword raised.
The pirates all drew back their
weapons, preparing to fight. But
instead of attacking, Tom bent his
knees and launched himself into the
air, somersaulting over their heads.

As he came out of the roll, Tom
threw up his shield, using the
power of Arcta's feather to slow
his fall. Tilting the shield, he glided
onwards, over workbenches and
startled slaves, until he reached
the lip of the pit. Then he angled
his shield sharply downwards, and
plunged into the shadowy darkness.

Tom landed in a crouch. Instantly,
his nostrils were filled with the
stench of putrid rotting meat

mingled with a vile musky scent, making him retch. As his eyes adjusted to the dimness, he could make out the dark bulk of a huge animal crouched over Daltec's fallen body. *Menox!*

The creature had mangy fur, stuck together in clumps, and a long bristly tail, which twitched eagerly as the Beast sniffed and pawed at the fallen wizard.

"Get away from him!" Tom cried. The Beast spun round with an angry hiss, rising up on his hind legs to stand three times as tall as a man. He glared back at Tom with bulbous red eyes, his forepaws raised, flexing scarlet metal claws.

As Tom took in the Beast's
grime-streaked, whiskered face
and tattered ears, he felt a surge

of disgust. *It's a gigantic rat!* The creature let out another furious hiss, revealing a single dagger-like tooth as long as Tom's sword, and made of the same red metal as his claws. *Redsteel!* Tom realised.

Through the red jewel in his belt, Tom heard the Beast's voice booming in his head.

It took four Beast Masters to take me down last time! A runt like you doesn't stand a chance. Leave me in peace to finish my meal.

In the shadows behind the Beast, Daltec shifted as if trying to rise, then sank back to the ground.

I have to get the Beast away from him, Tom thought.

And Menox's bragging had given him an idea.

Tom shrugged, touching the jewel, so Menox could understand him when he spoke. "Well, I've defeated over a hundred Beasts," he said. "Most of them were far bigger than you. And stronger."

Foolish boy! Menox hissed. *I will teach you a lesson.* The Beast sank on to all fours, powerful muscles bulging beneath his fur, then pounced, jaws wide and red claws bared.

Tom dived sideways, dodging the Beast's snapping teeth, then leapt across the pit, putting himself between Daltec and Menox. He turned to see the Beast gathering himself for another leap, red tooth glinting.

One hundred Beasts, and yet you run like a coward! hissed the giant rat.

A rowdy chant started up from above them. "Menox! Menox! Menox!" Tom glanced up to see the cruel grins and eager eyes of pirates crowded close together at the pit's edge.

Menox leapt, slashing for Tom's face with his long red claws. Tom blocked with his shield. The shock of the impact sent him hurtling through the air to land heavily on his back. He staggered to his feet, breathless, his shield arm weak with pain. The Beast's long snout snapped towards him, the single red tooth slicing through the air. Tom swung his sword, putting all the strength from his golden breastplate behind

it. Blade met tooth with a metallic clang, and Menox reeled back, eyes flashing with hatred.

Harsh voices shouted from above. "Finish him off!"

"Gut the landlubber brat!"

A dark missile streaked past Tom and clattered to the ground. More rocks followed, thrown by the watching pirates. Tom spotted a huge chunk of ore spinning towards him. He lifted his sword and smacked it aside. The rock hit Menox, bouncing off the creature's back. The Beast reared up with a furious hiss. Tom aimed the point of his sword at the Beast's exposed underbelly and dived forwards.

Suddenly, a heavy weight slammed into his shoulder from above.

"Got him!" a pirate cried as Tom stumbled and fell, his sword spinning from his numb fingers as he hit the dirt. He rolled on to his back, clutching his shoulder and gasping with pain. When he looked up, his eyes met those of the Beast, glaring down at him. The creature's hideous lipless mouth spread into a wide, evil grin and his fierce cry filled Tom's mind.

Now I shall tear your flesh from your bones!

BEAST ON THE RAMPAGE

Tom lay breathless with pain, his arm limp and useless. The chanting from above grew faster and louder, feverish with excitement. "Menox! Menox! Menox!" Through the agony that gripped him, Tom vaguely registered five deadly curved claws swiping his way. *Crack!* A flash

of white light blanked his vision.
Menox let out a furious screech,
and Tom caught the scent of singed
fur. He lifted his head to see the
hideous rat-Beast crouched in the
shadows, a raw red wound on his
shoulder where the fur had been
burned away. The pirates' chants
turned to boos and hisses as the
Beast curled in on itself, licking the
wound. Turning his head, Tom saw
Daltec standing now, his fingers still
crackling with magic as he lowered
his hands. The wizard's face looked
ashen and a long cut ran across his
forehead, but eyes were fierce.

"Here," Daltec said, holding out
Tom's sword in a shaking hand. Tom

took the blade, the feeling flowing back into his hand as the pain in his shoulder subsided.

"Thanks!" Tom said, scrambling to his feet. Daltec's eyes suddenly swam out of focus. He swayed. Tom quickly grabbed the wizard's arm, steadying him.

"Daltec! Over here!" Elenna's cry rose above the shouts of the pirates. Tom glanced towards the opposite edge of the pit to see her lowering a rope. He started to steer Daltec towards her, but the young wizard waved him away.

"I can make it..." Daltec croaked. "...the Beast..."

"Fight, fight, fight, fight!" the

pirates shouted, and Tom glanced around to see Menox crouching, ready to pounce once more. As Daltec hobbled away, Tom sank into a fighting stance and gritted his teeth. *I can do this*, he told himself.

Then he let out a battle cry, drew his sword and charged. Menox sprang for him at the same moment. Tom swung his sword, catching the creature mid-leap, raking his blade across Menox's muscled haunch.

Menox landed awkwardly on his injured limb. Tom jabbed for the Beast's side, piercing the thick hairy hide. As the Beast screeched in fury, new chants rang out from above, almost drowning out those of the

pirates. "Tom! Tom! Tom!"

Tom looked up to see slaves cheering him on, elbowing the pirates aside for a better view.

"Get out of there!" Elenna cried from the edge of the pit, with Daltec now beside her. Tom glanced at the hunched form of the Beast. A terrible rage burned in his eyes and, beneath his mangy singed fur, sinewy muscles flexed as he readied himself to spring.

Elenna's right! Tom realised. *I can't beat Menox down here – there's not enough room.* He turned and ran.

"Look out!" Elenna screamed. Tom glanced back to see a furious mass of dark fur, red eyes and slashing claws hurtling towards him. *No time to climb!* He called on the power of his golden boots and leapt… His stomach lurched – *I'm not going to make it!*

As he slammed towards the pit wall, he reached up as far as he could. His fingers just hooked over the edge of the pit. But he could already feel the dirt crumbling…

Firm hands closed about his wrists, yanking him up. Tom found himself standing between Elenna and Daltec at the edge of the pit, his heart thundering in his chest. Menox screeched and hissed in fury, his red claws raking the wall of the pit, right where Tom had been hanging. The Beast scrabbled frantically, trying to climb out, his eyes blazing. Tom glanced at the huge, tilted wooden cover for the pit, and then at the winch holding it up. The winch drum sat on the raised scaffold above them, reached by a ladder. Tom scrambled up the ladder, taking the rungs two at a time. He grabbed the winch handle and yanked. The crank barely moved. Screams of alarm rose up all around him. Tom looked down to see the crowd surging back from the edge of the pit as Menox's red-taloned claw groped over the edge.

Tom let go of the winch, drew

back his sword with both hands, then swiped for the thick chain with all his strength.

CLANG! The blow severed the chain, which whipped upwards with a metallic clatter. The pit cover fell with an echoing boom, trapping the Beast inside.

Tom breathed a sigh of relief.

A great cheer rang through crowd. "Tom! Tom!" But the cheers turned to cries of alarm when a terrific thud echoed up from the pit, the wooden lid jumping as the rat-Beast fought to get free.

Even a handful of pirates started to run, shoving through the crowd.

"Hold your ground!" One-Eye

shouted. "The Beast can't escape!"
But Tom could see doubt and fear in
the big man's single eye.

CRASH! Splintered planks of
wood exploded in every direction as
the pit cover burst open and Menox
scrambled out. One-Eye's face
drained of colour. He turned and
bolted, pushing a small girl out of
his way and sending her flying.

"Take cover!" Tom cried. Menox
let out a piercing screech, then
charged forward, claws lashing
right and left in fury as the villagers
and pirates fled. Young and old,
pirate and slave alike scrambled
together for safety, racing for the
mine tunnels or away from the

mountain towards open ground.
Menox swiped at benches and
scaffolding, sending rocks, tools and
crucibles filled with molten metal
flying.

"Tom! Look!" Elenna cried,
pointing towards the girl One-Eye

had pushed. A stream of spilled molten metal flowed towards her as she lay crying, her mouth wide and her palms grazed and bloody. A man and woman scrambled to reach her, their faces lined with horror, but Tom could see they'd never get to the girl in time. The scarlet metal smoked as it trickled towards the howling child. *She'll be maimed for life – or killed! I have to save her!*

THE HUNT
BEGINS

Calling on the power of his golden boots, Tom leapt from the platform and hurtled through the air to land in a crouch at the girl's side. He scooped her up and set her on her feet, out of the way of the deadly metal. "Run!" he told her. The girl's parents each took one of her hands and hurried her away.

Tom turned back to face the Beast. Some of the workers, including the sinewy old man who'd hit him, circled Menox, jabbing and slicing at the giant rat with redsteel blades. From her lookout on the raised

platform, Elenna fired arrow after arrow. Tom could see several shafts already sticking from the Beast's foul hide. But they didn't seem to be slowing him down. Nor did the bleeding cuts left by Tom's blade. *How can we beat him?* Then Tom remembered how the creature had recoiled from Daltec's energy spell in the pit. He glanced at the huge furnace at the centre of the worksite, still spewing dark smoke skywards. *Fire! Maybe that's the answer!*

"Elenna! Daltec!" Tom shouted. "I have an idea. Man the bellows and get the furnace as hot as you can. I need some serious flames!"

Elenna nodded. She and Daltec quickly climbed down from their platform and raced to the furnace with Tom.

Tom started to clamber quickly up the wooden scaffolding surrounding the structure. The terrible heat increased as he climbed until he could hardly breathe the scalding air. Finally, he reached the top. High wooden platforms suspended from a pulley cable carried buckets of ore from the breaking stations up to the circular chimney mouth. The platform beside Tom hung almost directly above the smoking hole. He leapt on to it, gasping at the sudden intense heat billowing up from

below. Then he put his hand to the
red jewel in his belt.

"Menox!" Tom cried, looking down
to where the Beast snapped and
slashed at the fighting slaves. The
giant rat lifted his glowing red eyes
to glare at Tom. "You told me you
would teach me a lesson. I am still
waiting!"

You will die! the Beast hissed
in his mind. With a flick of his
long, hairy tail, Menox sent the
slaves nearest to him flying. Then
he dropped down on to all fours
and bounded across the worksite
towards the furnace.

Yellow flames now replaced the
smoke coming from the chimney

mouth, thanks to Elenna and Daltec pumping at the handles of the huge leather bellows far below. The air shimmered around Tom in a searing heat haze. He felt dizzy and sick from the temperature and fumes, but he stood his ground. Below him, Menox reached the base of the scaffolding and, with the ease of a sewer rat climbing a drain, scampered upwards.

As the Beast reached the top of the scaffolding, Tom backed away, feeling the platform lurch as he moved. He gripped one of the chains suspending the platform from the pulley wheel above to steady himself. Menox smiled his hideous, red-toothed grin and leapt. The platform bucked as the huge rat landed on the far side with a hiss of triumph. Tom lifted his sword and hunkered down, as if ready to charge. But instead of attacking, Tom leapt up over the giant rat's head. Calling on the strength of his golden breastplate, he gripped hold of the chain attached to the far side of the platform, near where it met the pulley wheel, and tugged downwards with all his might. The platform tipped sharply. Menox let out a furious high-pitched screech and fell, scrabbling with his claws at the near-vertical wood, leaving deep gouges as he tried to cling on. The creature's eyes met Tom's for

one last time, filled with burning
hatred. Then Menox tumbled
straight into the chimney mouth,
disappearing into the flames.
Almost instantly, plumes of putrid
red-brown smoke poured from

the chimney mouth, billowing out
in every direction, making Tom's
eyes water and his breath catch in
his throat. He fought the terrible
nausea rising inside him, and clung
tight to the pulley chain.

When the reeking cloud had
passed, Tom let out a shaky breath
of relief, then slowly passed the
chain back through his hands, until
the platform below him levelled. As

he dropped down on to the wood
a chorus of cheers broke out from
the townsfolk below. His heart
swelled at the sound – Menox would
terrorise the people of Makai no
longer.

The Beast was defeated.

The sun setting over the mountains
of Makai cast an eerie red glow
over the landscape. Tom, Elenna
and Daltec sat together, watching
as Ria's freed slaves dismantled
everything that remained of the
metalworks.

Splintered wooden scaffolding
and pools of cooling red metal

covered the ground. The huge brick chimney at the centre of the site had been reduced to a pile of rubble, and more rubble filled the great pit where Menox had been held. Hundreds of workers still hacked at the remaining scaffolding and benches, smashing them to pieces. Tom noticed a small girl with dark curls picking her way across the rubble towards him. A shiny red blade glinted in her hand. As she reached Tom, she held out the object. *Menox's tooth!* Tom realised. And as he looked into the small girl's eyes, he recognised her as the child he'd saved.

"I found this among the bricks of

the furnace," the girl said. "You can have it as a present, as a thank you from all of us."

Tom smiled. "That's very kind of you," he said. "And it's exactly what I needed. A token from the Beast."

He took the blade, and tucked it into his belt as the young girl scurried away.

"You're going to hang for what you've done!" an angry voice shouted from behind Tom.

"You and every other pirate we catch," a female voice chimed in. Tom turned to see a group of workers striding from the mouth of a mine tunnel, dragging the bulky form of One-Eye between them. The pirate's wrists had been tied and blood stained his clothes. But he still wore a lazy smirk on his scarred and grime-streaked face.

Tom, Daltec and Elenna rose to meet the townsfolk and their captive.

"We're taking this one to the gallows," said the aged worker who'd hit Tom on the head.

"Surely you've seen enough death and suffering here," Tom said. "Killing pirates won't solve your problems. It will just leave blood on your hands. It would be far better to imprison them, or banish them from Makai."

One-Eye hawked and spat on the ground. "You really are as wet as you look, aren't you?" he said. "Next, you'll be telling them to send me off with a sack of food for the road! Well, you'll be taught your lesson soon enough. Ria's already stockpiled more than enough redsteel weapons to wipe out everyone in Avantia. Your days are numbered, boy."

"You sure you don't want him hanged?" the tall, grey-eyed woman holding One-Eye asked Tom.

Tom smiled. "Get him to help dismantle the forges. See how he likes being put to work." The villagers dragged One-Eye onwards, across the darkening worksite, leaving Tom alone with Elenna and Daltec.

"We'll have to go after her," Elenna said, in a weary voice. "We have to find out where she's stashed those weapons."

"And the other three Beasts she's woken," Daltec added.

Tom had a sudden idea, and hurried after the woman who was guarding One-Eye. "Actually, do you mind if we take this one?" he asked.

One-Eye looked alarmed. "Why? So you can torture me? I thought you didn't like bloodshed."

"We need a guide," said Tom. "Show us where Ria's gone."

"Never!" said One-Eye. "I'm no traitor." He sniffed. "Unless you're paying?"

Tom shook his head in contempt. "If you work for us honestly, I'll grant you your freedom when all this is over. How does that sound?"

The pirate leered. "When this is over you'll be dead, so Ria will free

me anyway. Deal."

Tom balled his fists and nodded.

"Ria is nothing but evil. While there's blood in my veins, I'm going to stop her, once and for all."

THE END

1

CONGRATULATIONS, YOU HAVE COMPLETED THIS QUEST!

At the end of each chapter you were awarded a special gold coin. The QUEST in this book was worth an amazing 8 coins.

Look at the Beast Quest totem picture inside the back cover of this book to see how far you've come in your journey to become

MASTER OF THE BEASTS.

The more books you read, the more coins you will collect!

Do you want your own Beast Quest Totem?

1. Cut out and collect the coin below
2. Go to the Beast Quest website
3. Download and print out your totem
4. Add your coin to the totem

www.beastquest.co.uk/totem

8

Don't miss the next exciting Beast Quest book, LARNAK THE SWARMING MENACE!

Read on for a sneak peek...

THE MOUNTAIN PASS

"I won't last until nightfall." One-Eye let out a pained groan as the makeshift wagon trundled over the rocky mountain path.

From beside him on the raised seat of the mule-drawn cart, Tom saw

Elenna roll her eyes. The pirate from Makai hadn't stopped complaining about the bumpiness of the road ever since they'd left Redsteel Forge.

Tom's hands tightened on the reins in his grasp, thinking that One-Eye could be a little bit more grateful. It was thanks to Tom and his friends that One-Eye had escaped at all. *So what if the ride is a little bumpy?* he thought. If the freed slaves of the forge had had their way, the pirate would have been executed on the spot. And Tom could hardly blame them – under Ria's harsh regime, they'd been beaten and starved as they toiled.

He gently flicked the mules' reins

as he urged the animals along a tricky part of the trail. He wiped away the sweat on his brow, thinking of the Quest ahead. *If that prisoner hadn't washed up on Avantian*

shores, we'd never have known about the four ancient Beasts Ria awoke, Tom thought. Now it was up to him and his friends to stop her from using those Beasts to invade Avantia.

The cart clattered over another big rock.

"Ouch!" One-Eye howled.

Daltec sighed from his position next to the former gangmaster. "I thought Makai pirates were the toughest around."

Elenna snorted with laughter.

Tom looked over his shoulder to see One-Eye scowling at the young wizard. "We don't all have magic to cushion ourselves," he mumbled.

Tom tutted. "Daltec would never waste his magic on making himself more comfortable. Not when there are far better uses for his powers."

"Like defeating Ria?" One-Eye questioned.

"Exactly," Daltec replied. "With Elenna's skill, Tom's bravery and my magic, Ria will be defeated."

"Yet somehow, my mistress got away." One-Eye was smirking. "And her plan to invade and conquer Avantia moves one step closer, while your so-called Quest appears to be failing."

Elenna whipped round in her seat. "Has the cart ride knocked the sense from your head?" she asked.

"We defeated her Beast Menox the Sabre-Toothed Terror, halted her production of redsteel weapons, and freed the innocent people forced to work for her. Our Quest is going just fine."

One-Eye scoffed. "One Beast! Ria has others, and more clever plans than you could ever imagine."

"Just ignore him, Elenna,"Tom said. "In this heat, we need to save our energy."

Elenna's jaw was still clenched, but she nodded and faced the path ahead.

Tom was grateful for his friend's determination. They would need it. Ria was young but she definitely took after her parents, Kensa and Sanpao, when it came to ruthlessness and scheming. She ran at the first sign of trouble, but knew how to make even worse trouble at every turn. He touched the blade-like tooth tucked into his belt, a token won for defeating Menox. *I've defeated Ria before; I'll do it again...*

As they reached the bottom of the mountain pass, dusk fell. The way ahead forked into two separate rocky paths and Tom realised that the mules would struggle to go much further. He pulled on the reins. "We'll travel the rest of the way on foot," he said.

"But which direction will you

choose?" One-Eye asked. "I can lead you straight to Ria if you wish...for a price, of course."

Tom raised an eyebrow. One-Eye cast a pitiful figure with his bruises and scratches and the magical manacles that Daltec had conjured for his wrists. The pirate also seemed jumpy, his gaze darting to the left part of the fork and then back again.

"You're not exactly in a position to make deals," Tom pointed out. "You're our prisoner and you'll be paid in our protection from any Beasts we meet." Tom and Elenna cut the mules loose. "Besides, I know which way Ria has gone. You keep on looking at the path on the left."

One-Eye glowered but said
nothing. They walked on, soon
coming to another path that tracked
along the base of the mountain

before slanting upwards and passing through it.

"The way through the mountain is narrow," Daltec said, peering ahead.

"It's not supposed to be easy, is it, Avantian?" One-Eye scoffed. "That's the way of Makai. The roads here are treacherous to any who don't know them."

"Sounds about right," Elenna muttered. "An island made up of cutthroats with an equally cutthroat landscape."

They entered the narrow mountain passage, One-Eye leading the way.

"You know, in the good old days, these mountain paths were crawling with outlaws as fierce as lions." One-

Eye's voice echoed off the sides of the walkway. "Bandits would stand as still and quiet as statues, wearing clothes that blended in with the rock face so they could ambush the unsuspecting." One-Eye suddenly stumbled and began to curse.

"Then I guess you can't be related to any of them," Elenna mused. "I mean, you're useless at staying quiet."

Read
LARNAK THE SWARMING MENACE
to find out what happens next!

Fight the Beasts,
Fear the Magic

Do you want to know more
about BEAST QUEST?
Then join our Quest Club!

Visit
www.beastquest.co.uk/club
and sign up today!

OUT NOW!

The epic adventure is brought
to life on **Xbox One** and **PS4**
for the first time ever!

www.maximumgames.com   www.beast-quest.com